Happy Valentine's Day, Dolores

Barbara Samuels

Melanie Kroupa Books
Farrar, Straus and Giroux ◆ New York

For my mom

Library of Congress Cataloging-in-Publication Data
Samuels, Barbara.
    Happy Valentine's Day, Dolores / Barbara Samuels.— lst ed.
        p. cm.
    Summary: Dolores has agreed to stop "borrowing" things from her older sister Faye's
dresser, but then she discovers a special Valentine's Day necklace there.
    ISBN-13: 978-0-374-32844-3
    ISBN-10: 0-374-32844-7
    [1. Conduct of life—Fiction. 2. Sisters—Fiction. 3. Necklaces—Fiction.
4. Valentine's Day—Fiction.] I. Title.

PZ7.S1925Har 2006
[E]—dc22

                                                                        2004040463

Most of the time Dolores and her big sister, Faye, got along just fine.

But Dolores had a habit . . .

of sneaking into Faye's room . . .

and borrowing a few things.

Finally Faye decided she'd had enough.

NEVER AGAIN!

For three whole days the sisters didn't speak to each other.

"Duncan," said Dolores, "would you mind asking Faye to please pass the ketchup?"

For weeks Dolores didn't go near Faye's things. But one night she saw Faye slip a small box into her dresser drawer.

"One teeny peek couldn't hurt," she thought.

Inside the box was a frog. But not just any frog. It was a special Valentine's Day frog necklace. When you pressed a button on its tummy, it croaked a sweet little tune.

"Wow!" said Dolores. "Aren't you something."

Then she heard Faye's footsteps in the hall.
"Got to put you back now, froggie," whispered Dolores,
"or I'll be in big trouble!"

KEEP
OUT!

The next day at school Dolores couldn't stop thinking about that frog. Valentine's Day was only two days away. Was Faye going to give the frog to her best friend, Martha?

Or had some *boy* given it
to Faye, Dolores wondered.

After school, while Faye was at soccer practice, Dolores took out the necklace.

"Don't look at me like that!" she said to Duncan.

"I just want to try it on— is that a crime?

"Boy, this clasp is tricky!

"It's not like I'm stealing it. I'll put it right back!

"There! Doesn't it look pretty?"

But then the front door slammed—FAYE!

There was no time to take off the necklace. Dolores shoved the box back in the drawer, ran downstairs, and covered her neck.

"How was soccer?" she asked Faye, trying to sound casual.

"Okay," said Faye.

The necklace was even harder to take off than it was to put on. Dolores wore it for the rest of the day.

"Do you have a sore throat?" asked Faye at dinner.

At bedtime Duncan accidentally pressed the button on the frog. "What was that?" asked Faye.

"Duncan has the hiccups," said Dolores. "I'll get him some water."

In the bathroom, Dolores finally figured out how to open the clasp of the necklace. But then she changed her mind.

"If I wear the frog to school tomorrow, I can show it to Shirley," Dolores whispered to Duncan. "I'll put it back after school, and Faye will never know the difference."

The next day Dolores showed the necklace to Shirley.
She knew her best friend would never tell.

"Who gave you that?" whispered Shirley.

"A secret admirer," said Dolores.

It wasn't long before . . .   everybody knew that . . .   Dolores had a boyfriend . . .

who'd given her a frog.

"That's quite enough!" said the music teacher, Ms. Sharp. She removed the necklace.

"It shall be returned to you, Dolores, at the end of class when you have written the sentence 'Frogs do not belong in music' thirty times."

Dolores was up to sentence number twenty-seven when Faye and another sixth grader came into the room.

"We're the milk monitors for the week," said Faye. "We baked these special Valentine's Day cupcakes for the music class." She smiled at Dolores.

After school Dolores raced home with the frog in her pocket. "Faye really is a *very* nice sister," she thought. "If I get home in time, I promise *I will never ever borrow any of her things again!*"

"Phew!" said Dolores.
"I made it!" She greeted
 Duncan with a big hug . . .

and a twirl . . .

and ran up to the bedroom.

But when she reached inside her pocket . . .

NO FROG!

"It must have fallen out on the way home,"
thought Dolores. "What can I do?"

Then she had an idea.
Dolores took the money she'd been
saving for a special treat.

She got the empty necklace box from Faye's drawer. It said
HEARTS ETC. "That's next door to the animal hospital
where we take Duncan," thought Dolores, "only a few minutes
away by cab. But I can't take a cab without a grownup unless
it's an emergency . . . Hmmm . . .

"Here, Duncan!" she called sweetly.

"I'm so sorry, Duncan, but you've had a serious accident . . .

and you simply must see a doctor . . .

IMMEDIATELY!"

"TAXI!

"Emergency! BROADWAY ANIMAL HOSPITAL—and step on it!"

"Poor thing!" said the driver, looking at Duncan.

"Now, that was easy, wasn't it?" said Dolores to Duncan. "And this will just take a minute."

"You're a lucky girl," said the saleslady. "This is the very last froggie necklace we have in stock."

"Now everything's going to be all right," thought Dolores. "I have just enough money for cab fare home and two balloons."

But Duncan had other ideas.
"Come back here!" yelled Dolores.

"Who needs a cab?" thought Dolores, as she paid Mr. Ying
for the damage. "It's a beautiful day—I'll walk!"

But suddenly the day
was not quite so beautiful.

"What happened to *you*?" asked Faye
when Dolores and Duncan finally got home.

"Oh, we had a little emergency," said Dolores,
"but it's all okay now."

That night, while Faye was asleep, Dolores
slipped the box with the new necklace into Faye's
top drawer.

"Go back to Faye where you belong, you naughty
bad-luck froggie!" whispered Dolores.

But the next morning when she came downstairs, there was a familiar-looking box next to her cereal bowl.

"Happy Valentine's Day!" said Faye.

"For *me*?" stammered Dolores.

"I'm glad it's a surprise," said Faye. "The funny thing is, yesterday I found this necklace at the bottom of the stairs."

"You did?" said Dolores.

"The empty box was on my bed," said Faye. "So I put the frog back inside and hid it in my closet."

"Really?" said Dolores.

"But then," said Faye, "when I opened my drawer this morning . . .

"There's a very simple explanation," said Dolores.

"What's that?" asked Faye.

Dolores thought for a few seconds.
Then she smiled and said . . .

"HAPPY VALENTINE'S DAY, FAYE!"